THE DINNER LADY
and other stories

THE DINNER LADY
and other stories

Ann Renard

Matador
9 Priory Business Park,
Wistow Road, Kibworth Beauchamp,
Leicestershire. LE8 0RX
Tel: 0116 279 2299
Email: books@troubador.co.uk
Web: www.troubador.co.uk/matador
Twitter: @matadorbooks

ISBN 978 1788032 735

British Library Cataloguing in Publication Data.
A catalogue record for this book is available from the British Library.

Printed and bound in the UK by TJ International, Padstow, Cornwall
Typeset in 12pt Minion Pro by Troubador Publishing Ltd, Leicester, UK

Matador is an imprint of Troubador Publishing Ltd

FOR MY GRANDCHILDREN
Isla, Emma, Tilly and Sam

CONTENTS

About the Author

Ann Renard previously ran her own business as a dance teacher. She then changed direction to teach and assess people with various physical, mental and learning needs. Ann is now retired and is based in Warwickshire. She has two grown-up children and four grandchildren.

The Dinner Lady and Other Stories is her first book to be published. The characters in each story are brought to life with plenty of humour and a touch of fantasy.

THE ANTIQUES DEALER

Lesley stood at the back of the auction room, brochure in hand.

He was interested in the Goldscheider figure of a maiden, Lot 205. She was beautiful. Her golden, softly adorned body, curved slightly to the left as she held a green vase between her right shoulder and regal head. Her calf muscles were high, her naked toes painted and perfect between braided sandals. She was poised on the statuette, waiting, waiting for whoever claimed her as his own. He wanted to take the weight from her shoulders and let her body rest along the length of his arm.

He let the first few items on sale pass him by, then threw in a bid for a Lalique leaf and frosted glass vase. Good, the auctioneer had spotted him at the back of the room. Now again for the Meakin Jug – 'stop Lesley, carefully does it, stop at £60 before you go past the estimated bid,' he cautioned himself.

He weighed the crowd up. Most of the bids were reaching a good price, with seven or eight bidders interested in the much better stuff. The chipped or broken items were way down in value, even the William de Morgan and Clarice Cliff.

The catalogue valuation for the Goldscheider was between £500-£700. He would wait until the bidding started and got past £300. Lesley inched around the side of the room to get nearer to the front. It was an unusually large crowd today, unexpected when you considered the current climate. Unfortunately his left shoulder started to twitch, a habit he couldn't shake off.

Two or three people started the bid; £100, £130, £200, going up.

He looked over to his right to see a smartly dressed woman taking instructions on her mobile phone. She was concentrating on the caller and dropped her head to listen.

"£220" – "young man in the centre."

"£280" – the auctioneer repeated "lady on the phone."

Now; – go for it Lesley – brochure in the air – "£300!"

"£300 – gentleman in the brown cord jacket in from my right."

Hold back again.

"£400 – lady with telephone bid to my side left," the auctioneer indicated again towards the smart lady in the grey suit.

Lesley felt the sweat trickle down the back of his shirt, his jacket felt hot and cumbersome on his thickly-set body, he needed to be on his toes now. Hold back, stay calm.

"£430 young gentleman – centre – baton 54."

Crikey! Lesley looked from left to right, he had to have her. He was prepared to go to the top, he put his hand into his pocket fingering the notes.

"£500!" he called out. He smirked, he would show them he was a serious contender.

"I have £500 from the gentleman my right, any more bids on this lovely lady?

Lesley looked slyly towards the lady on the phone, she had her head down and was concentrating on the speaker.

"Going – going—"

"£800" – she held the phone in the air.

Lesley opened his mouth aghast, wiping the sweat now trickling from his hair into his eyes with the back of his sleeve. He shuffled back a few inches, all eyes on him, the twitch to his left shoulder started to irritate. He held his right hand over his arm and dropped his catalogue. He bent to retrieve it with a grunt.

"GONE. The telephone bid, lady side-left." The auctioneer pointed, she raised her hand accepting the deal and started to move away. Lesley watched helplessly as the assistants started to wrap his beautiful figurine in bubble wrap.

He left the room and shuffled round to the back of the building. The assistants for Chartwell-Mason auctioneers were piling ladder-back chairs, an Ercol dining table and a Gordon Russell walnut and mahogany desk from the previous sale, into vans for transport. Packing boxes and blankets were strewn across the yard.

He stood behind a packing crate, holding his gut. Perhaps he would see the woman in the grey suit leave the building, maybe she would negotiate?

He hurried to the front in time to see her handing the figurine to the driver, swing her long legs into the Mercedes and retrieve her trophy, before giving the chauffeur instructions to drive away.

Lesley opened the front door of his 1930's semi-detached house, pushing it against the free standing oak coat-rack with mirror. He put the brochure to the right on the washstand, avoiding the commemorative jug and bowl and squeezed through the gap to the Marley tiled kitchen and scullery at the back, to take off his shoes. The hole in the sole of his right shoe indicated they had seen better days, but he didn't like spending his money on unnecessary things.

He put on his slippers and made himself a cup of tea.

He would have the Wall's steak pie for tea, with some bread and margarine, he had a tin of fruit cocktail and carnation milk for pudding.

He cheered up a little. Maybe he would get his figurine back sometime? They often did the rounds and could turn up at another sale. He would keep his eyes open.

On Monday morning he walked to work. Walking through the lower-level car-park with its reserved spaces for library staff, he entered through the 'basement door for staff-only' at 8.30am. He turned off the alarms and unlocked the front doors, putting the bolt on which he would draw back to open to the public at 9.30am.

Julie and Suri arrived at 8.55 and asked him if he had enjoyed his day off on Friday. He said he had enjoyed it and 'had they missed him at the library?'

Julie rolled her eyes at Suri,

"Yes of course we did, we missed your cheerful conversation Les."

Suri said she had no one to turn to when she couldn't get the computers to log on.

He was never sure with these young girls, he thought they were teasing him. They talked about their 'partners' and how they were 'out of their heads' at the weekend.

He checked all the books and periodicals had been correctly replaced from the weekend returns and the journals and newspapers were available on the low reading tables. He checked that the 'for reference only' books were in correct order.

He wasn't very good at the desk or with the customers. But if anyone asked him, he knew exactly where a book was, he could quote the shelf and reference number, the publishers, even the ISBN number!

He had watched Suri carefully at the desk and saw how she smiled at the customers. It seemed easy enough, but somehow when he smiled they didn't respond in quite the same way.

He liked the old maps and limited edition books best, in the dark room below the library, kept under lock and key. It was strange, he seemed able to memorise the symbols and details of the maps in his head.

He looked at Suri from the corner of his eye. He edged over to the front desk as she prepared to locate something on the computer for an elderly gentleman. She looked like his Goldsheida figure, soft brown silken arms and graceful legs. He watched her fingers as she logged-in as S.Kadesh. He looked away hurriedly as she scowled at him. The twitch in his left shoulder started up again, sometimes it seemed to move up into his face.

He would go back to the Auction room and ask Mr Mason.

"Lot 205 Mr Smith? I expect that was Mr Kadesh. He's very keen on figurines. We've a Kitchen and Paraphernalia sale coming up soon Mr Smith, or the Furniture sale – now you've always done well there," Mr Mason reassured.

Lesley turned to go home an idea beginning to take shape, he would replace some of the old furniture at the weekend. He hadn't touched a thing since his mother had passed away 8 years ago. Mother always said – "quality not quantity." He would start with his bedroom.

On Saturday he walked purposefully out of the back door and down the garden path to the garage. He pushed open the flaking, wooden side door. The green Morris Minor sat there. He usually walked to work but kept the tank half full, just in case. He switched on his father's Bush transistor radio on the top of the work bench at the front, smiling to himself as it crackled into life. He reached behind it for the axe, placing it carefully next to the hammer on the top of the work bench. He went upstairs and angled his now empty chest of drawers down the stairs walking it out of the kitchen, down the garden path and into the garage, followed closely by the single divan bed. He moved the lawn roller, trug and washboard to the side and smashed the furniture to pieces.

He loosened the handbrake and (careful of the AA sign) pushed the car forwards, loaded up the boot and breathed heavily. At twenty miles an hour the journeys to the tip took a little longer than expected. But he managed it all before they closed.

It was a good quality furniture sale. He went for the double bed, with Jacobean oak headrest in the art nouveau style showing the metamorphosis of a woman rising from a lake, surrounded by a bed of water lilies. No 'Mr Kadesh' to beat him this time, Lesley smiled to himself holding down his left shoulder. Mr Louis (Mr Mason's personal assistant) looked towards him and tapped his nose.

"Yours Mr Smith, double thickness bubble wrap again? We'll transport the bed in the lorry for you at no extra charge."

The holiday period was coming up. Julie and Suri went to places like Thailand or Croatia. They seemed relieved when he said he wouldn't need a holiday just some occasional days off.

He told the girls he was decorating his kitchen.

"I like Ikea," Julie had said.

"Mobens do good kitchens," Suri added.

Lesley didn't want a burglary or break-in now that his house was taking shape. The local locksmith had some old cast iron locks with big keys, and you could lock the door from both the inside and out. He would get two. One for the front and one for the back door.

The Jewellery sale was coming up. It had caused a few problems with Julie and Suri when he announced he was taking two days off to attend; Tuesday and Wednesday!

"You know I'm away on my holidays on Wednesday." Julie complained. "The flight leaves at 7 o'clock in the morning. We're not allowed to leave Suri on her own, it's company policy. I think you're being selfish Lesley."

"It's ok," Suri said pacifyingly. "Maybe we can ask someone to come and stand in from central branch? You know Lesley doesn't get a proper holiday Julie, he often goes without."

"Well I'm not sorting it," sulked Julie.

"I'll do it," Lesley volunteered, "I have left it a bit late after all," he admitted.

If he actually 'forgot' to ask someone from Central branch; he would have to come in. That would leave just him and Suri.

"Try a washing day on one of your days off – Lesley," Julie suggested fanning her hand over her nose.

On Tuesday Lesley was first in line. He bought a Georg Jenson brooch and Lapis Lazuli ring. He bought a Liberty & Co gem set pendant and earrings designed by Koppel. He paid in cash. He bought red-roses for the Wedgwood vase. All ready now.

On Wednesday he drove to the library, reversing into a space right next to the basement door.

He put up a sign on the front door on a piece of A4 paper, pocketing the large roll of sellotape.

Library closed for training.
Apologies for any inconvenience

At 5.20pm Lesley returned to the front doors and removed the notice, checking the alarms were switched on and the overnight lights on the timer.

He drove home slowly, parking the Morris Minor right up by the workbench, closing the garage doors from inside. It had been a struggle but the boot had been just big enough.

Mr Kadesh would surely make the exchange, he consoled himself as he made his way up the garden path, struggling with the large, wriggling, bubble-wrapped package, in the heavy duty, extra-large, garden-refuse bag. But, maybe this time he should move on? Expand his tastes a little, get with it? After all, he had bought all the jewellery, bedroom furniture and new kitchen equipment to make it more like a home. Another idea was beginning to take shape in his mind.

His left shoulder began to shake, his eye and his cheek started to twitch as he laid his parcel down and inserted his key into the back-door with shaking hands.

THE APPOINTED PERSON

"After an accident, if your casualty is bleeding profusely, with a continuous flow of blood from the left arm, what would you do?"

The attractive young black girl, in navy blue trousers and a white tunic answered confidently: "Apply pressure, elevate and ask him if he would like to sit down. Reassure – and get someone to call for an ambulance. Be prepared to treat for shock."

Matt looked to his left arm, his head throbbing. He had another 4 hours and 30 minutes of this torture to go through.

At first, they had introduced themselves and said why they were on the course. There were people from all professions; carers, dental nurses, sports coaches. Fortunately that had taken up half an hour and hadn't been too difficult.

Then they had discussed different types of emergencies and how to call the emergency services with explicit details of the casualties; sex, age, apparent injuries.

They had talked about small burns to the surface of the skin and immersion in cold water for ten minutes, followed by treatment for severe burns. He had imagined his fingers numb with the excruciating pain of shreds of skin hanging from his finger tips and his nails charred and shrivelled. That was bad enough.

But this was worse, much worse. As he looked over towards the instructor, Mrs Perry, he imagined he saw blood spread across her chest as it flowed out of a ripped vein, turning the once cream jumper to a torn, cloggy brown mess. It was all too much, but somehow he just had to get through this course if he wanted to take his group away for the Outdoor/ Activity week. He had managed to avoid the First-Aid at work course last year, his first probationary year in teaching, but there was no avoiding it this year. There were two male and two female members of staff going to Hay-on-Wye, with forty pupils from the 6th form. They were camping in a forest, kayaking, rock climbing and abseiling. All the staff had to be first-aid trained in case they were separated from one another and they had to deal with emergencies. The other three had completed their 1 day course within the last three years. It was all just common sense they said – but to him, this was one day of sheer torture. If he could just get through this, he would not have to undergo this day in hell for another three years.

Last week, he had spent an hour or two every evening, trying to prepare himself for the dreaded day. He read 'if one has a phobia, gradual exposure to the object or circumstance causing the phobia helps one come to terms with it.' No such luck. In the safety of his own flat he had looked up information on first-aid on the internet. But no matter how often he had read through Cardio-Pulmonary Resuscitation; compression depth and rescue breath, he felt faint. He had forced himself to watch 'A night in A&E' and 'Holby City'. Then programs on cosmetic surgery; straightening bent penises, increasing breast sizes, removing unsightly veins. At the end of each, he would be lying on the rug in front of the TV rocking and groaning in agony with a sick bowl nearby. He hadn't slept well for the last three days.

"Hello Mr Carey, are you OK? You look a little pale. You're not going to pass out on us are you?" Mrs Perry asked him cheerfully.

Oh please! Please don't draw attention to me. I am trying to pretend the fear is out there in another entity and I can cope with it. I am merely watching from the sidelines as the person who feels sick and faint is forcing himself to get through the next four hours and five minutes. The 'detachment technique' is ruined. My cover is blown, brought to the attention of the whole group, now I will definitely pass out.

All eyes were fixed on him.

"Who me? Fine thanks," he said in a high pitched voice. His hands shook visibly as he refilled his plastic beaker from the 'aqua-water' container in the corner of the room. He had already refilled it half a dozen times already.

"Perhaps – you could be our body for this situation then – sit on the floor," she commanded.

No, no he did not want inclusion. Sod off! He

would rather be anywhere than in this room right now.

"Er – ok."

At least he would get to sit on the floor which would stop him from dropping down there. Maybe he could lie down and shut his eyes to stop the flashing lights and they would just think he was a good actor.

They cleared a space for him on the carpet-tiled floor. The practising first-aider put on disposable gloves and applied pressure on the arm directly on the injury. She then held it in an elevated position and wrapped bandages one on top of the other as apparently the first bandage was now coated in blood.

OMG it was getting worse. Mrs Perry was talking about a piece of glass sticking up from the arm and applying bandages around this dagger, not on top of it, as you could push the glass further into the arm! He took a look at his left arm at the sharp piece of glass which had now apparently lodged itself under the first and second layer of skin. The wretched wound was wrenched apart showing tendons and muscles slashed to pieces. He groaned inwardly, and reached into his trouser pocket to draw his handkerchief out and wipe it across his sweating forehead.

Mrs Perry turned her attention to Matt writhing on the floor, now a very grey colour, his eyes tightly shut.

"Right class, now lets demonstrate the position for shock," she sing-songed cheerfully.

"Sonia, could you just collect the blanket from the desk? Rolled-up coats will do – and we elevate the feet – so." He opened his eyes slightly as Sonia, a personal trainer from a gym in the high street, gently knelt over him and softly slid a folded jumper under his head.

"Now if our casualty passes out and becomes unconscious then we put him in the recovery position. I will demonstrate with Mr Carey here, then after coffee I want you all to have a go on each other."

Matt was aware of the enemy turning him onto his side with his hand resting under his cheek and his upper leg bent at an angle to keep his body from rolling backwards or forwards. He was vaguely aware of the other eleven people walking around him, checking his pulse and lifting his chin so that his airway was open.

Mrs Perry invited them all to take a comfort break and return in 10 minutes.

"Don't rush to get up Matt."

As if!

He slowly sat up and put his hand to his throbbing head, the room was spinning and he wanted desperately to go to the toilet. He shifted himself onto his hands and knees and using a table close by, pulled himself slowly upwards to stand.

In the corner of the room Mrs Perry was sorting through her handouts, with her back to him.

"OK?" she asked cheerfully, without turning round.

"Yes fine," he left the room to relieve himself holding onto the wall above the urinal. After washing his cold hands in hot water, then mopping his sweating brow with cold water; he poured himself a coffee with four sugars from the coffee vending machine and clung onto the beaker as he walked slowly back to his chair. He squeezed the plastic beaker so hard that the boiling liquid spilt over his hand. Mrs Perry rushed him to the 'aqua-water' pushing his hand under the siphon.

"Thank you Matt, it looks like you're prepared to demonstrate all the accidents today!" she joked.

During the next hour everyone practised the tasks set out on the board, including blowing air into some life size pink doll smelling of dettol, referred to fondly as 'Annie'. He was OK when he was moving around and focusing, even trying to find pulses in peoples necks or their wrist. He felt sure he would manage the next ten minutes before lunch, then he was half way through the day.

"If your casualty is in the recovery position – and you suspect an injured lung how would you lie your casualty on their side?" she tested.

"If the blood is bright red and frothy, you would put the injured lung to the floor," Oliver, the lab-technician replied.

Oh God, no. Perhaps he wouldn't get to the lunch break. In fact, would he ever be able to work if he had to go through all of this in real life?

Biology was NOT his subject. Physics was his subject – logical and predictable. Sport was his passion and he coached a good game of soccer. He had so looked forward to it, but he wouldn't offer to go on the Outdoor Program again.

"Could you pass those handouts around, Mr Carey?" Mrs Perry dropped them on the floor, accidentally? Matt bent down to pick them up, as he did so he felt the blood rush back to flush his face.

"Look through your notes over lunch break and we'll do fractures and sprains when you return. Shall we say, in 30 minutes?"

Matt wondered if he should go home. He had parked his car in the multi-storey carpark two blocks away. He could say he had had an urgent phone call and leave now.

Just as he was about to leg-it, she called after him.

"Ah Mr Carey, just the man. Would you mind bringing the skeleton in for me from the cupboard under the stairs?"

"Er – I was going to pop out and buy myself some lunch," he lied.

"No time for that I'm afraid, we've lots to get through. Didn't you get the email about bringing in a packed lunch? Here, share mine. I got a Lunch Deal as I came in this morning and it has three sandwiches and a piece of carrot cake. I shouldn't have bought it," she said, patting her rounded stomach. You'll be doing me a favour."

She busied herself with slings and antiseptic wipes as Matt brought in a large case then unlocked it pulling out "Charlie." He hung him up on a coat-stand by means of the hook driven into his skull, straightening out protruding skeletal limbs as he did so.

The rest of the group returned in good spirits and Mrs Perry hurtled straight into fractures. It appeared you just had to support these days and call an ambulance. He would be OK with that, no blood and gore. Sprains needed a sling, ok – he could tie one around his partners' opposite shoulder. So far so good.

Now choking. She took his arm and turned his back to the group and located an area between his shoulder blades and slapped five times. The group seemed to be enjoying the fact that he was a constant puppet. It even made him smile a little. Epileptic fits were not choking and were not to be treated as such. Although they could choke during a fit, apparently.

One hour to go.

He survived Heart Attacks and Strokes by focussing on Sonia's black shorts with a pink stripe down the side, matching her pink trainers.

Then – Oh Joy! they could leave when they had answered the written tests. Time to go, free at last. First to finish. He swung round to take his jacket from the back of his chair. Oh no! She was calling him over from table desk at the front. Don't say he had failed the practical. He couldn't go through all of this again.

"Matt," she said quietly, putting her hand on his arm. "I usually find the sensitive ones like you take it all in and deal with real emergencies far better than those who think they know it all. Well done for getting through the day. The first time is always the worst, it sometimes comes as a bit of a shock to realise that a life and death threat is real and people can survive with a good first-aider to hand. It won't be nearly as bad next time, I promise," she said with a smile.

Next time! No way. He'd rather resign if he had to go through all of that again.

As he left the building in search of the car-park, he allowed his thoughts to drift back through the last year.

Maybe if the paramedics had arrived sooner, his father would have survived the heart attack? Or – perhaps if he had been around he would have been able to help? Fifty-four. Fifty four wasn't old enough for his Dad to go. He had been so fit, a cricket and football player like himself. He wiped a tear from his eye. How he missed him.

He needed a drink. He had a couple of beers in the flat. Not advised in the case of shock, but a bit of self medication was called for today. He might even watch 'Casualty' tonight. Now that was a first, 'Casualty' – not the beer.

THE BAG LADY

Marcia tucked her shoulder length, dark blonde hair behind her ears and reached inside her Marc Jacobs bag to retrieve her Smartphone.

"Hi Justin, I'm on my way to get some lunch," she recorded, "when I get back we'll go over the list of applicants and reassess their suitability for the post." Pause.

"At the interview, I'll ask them to identify the current gaps in the health and social care provisions for the elderly." Pause.

"I will then ask how they see us filling those gaps. I expect them to have done their research and the answer to be a 'Maximillion Home'. With reasons why they have reached that decision." Pause.

"Could you add that to the interview questions and fill in the expected responses? Thanks Justin." Snap.

Marcia dropped the phone into her bag and lifted her left hand to check her silver Armani earrings were in place. They were. She smoothed her hands over her size 10 black pencil skirt and pressed the green crossing button in front of her.

She waited for the flashing green man, noticing people on the other side of the road: business people on their lunch breaks; a teenager – reading his text messages, a mother holding the hands of twin girls. They would be about seven or eight, the girls. Melanie's age, her fun loving beautiful twin sister – before – before.

Marcia reached the other side of the road. She took a deep breath, relax and control, relax and control.

It was busy in the town centre, a crisp sunny day with a definite nip in the spring air, but maybe a few dark clouds over there, on the horizon.

She walked towards the raised platform of the clock tower in the centre of the market place. Nearly there – "Oh Shit!"

She fell headlong over a stuffed black bin liner in the gutter. She looked down at her hands, grit and dirt were embedded in the palms, further down a pair of threadbare tights hung off her slim legs and a once shiny pair of black-heeled court shoes, now dangled on her feet, scuffed at the toes.

She looked up and saw an old lady sitting on the top step just under the clock, Her head was turned at an angle to her body and she was peering down at her.

"Is this your stupid rubbish?" Marcia barked as she pulled herself to her feet and kicked the plastic bin bag emptying more of its contents, food wastes and papers onto the pavement, directly underneath the clock tower.

The old lady watched her. She edged her body slowly round and straightened her creaking neck and back. Then fixing her grey eyes on Marcia's face: "I beg your pardon ma'am, were you talking to me?" she asked softly yet firmly, with an American twang to her voice.

"Yes, I said is this your stupid bag" Marcia replied, a little less forcibly .

The old lady leaned forward, peered at the bag from under the netting on her hat, then leaned back neatly crossing one foot over the other. Marcia looked at her varicosed feet, noticing the knarled and bent toe peeping out from a pair of shiny black patent shoes, with what must have been a three inch stiletto heel. The old lady lifted the net away from her black pillar-box hat, releasing a mass of straggling grey hair.

"Why – of course not, do I look as though I own that bag of – garbage?"

The old lady leant down and with a long spike on the end of her black laced umbrella poked the bag and its contents into the gutter. Returning her grey eyes to Marcia she looked her up and down, her gaze stopping at the torn tights and scuffed hands.

She then proceeded to slowly remove the black leather gloves from her wizened old hands, each finger released slightly from their grip as she gently worked them away. Caressing the gloves, she placed them beside her Hermes handbag. She leant over to the smaller of the two square, brown leather suitcases, tucked tidily by her side. Balancing this on her knees, she clicked it open, lifted the lid and took out a green Bakelite flask, two embroidered handkerchiefs, a red cardboard box of 'lifebuoy soap' and a pink tin.

She unscrewed a cup from the top of the flask and carefully poured scalding water.

"Here, dab the handkerchief – mind your fingers now, and use the lifebuoy to clean up your wound."

The smell of the carbolic soap had Marcia reeling, but she did as she was told. Sucking in her breath, she dabbed and cleaned her hands and knees.

"Now pat it dry with the other 'kerchief then put on some Germolene. You'll soon feel better and as right as rain," she said passing Marcia the pink tin. The skin on her aged hands was almost transparent, showing veins beneath the surface, her knuckles bent and distorted.

Marcia straightened. "Thanks," she said awkwardly, handing back the handkerchiefs.

"No honey – keep them, I have plenty. In fact you'll be needing stockings, those are a dis–saster" as she opened the larger case. Leaning forward she took out a packet of 'Pretty Polly Sheer Silk Stockings'.

"Of course you'll have one of these," she said as she discretely showed Marcia a lacy corset and suspender belt from between layers of cashmere jumpers and silken petticoats.

Marcia's eyes opened wide, "Wow, are you like into vintage?" she asked taken aback.

"Oh goodness gracious no, I hate all that old fashioned stuff," the old lady chortled as she smoothed her full black and white skirt over her pronounced petticoats, tightening a red belt around a nipped-in waistline and brushed an imaginary speck off her fitted black travelling jacket.

"I do like Dior but I prefer Hartnell. Didn't Elizabeth look lovely in her wedding dress? And now she has those two darling children."

"I'm sorry?" questioned Marcia.

"Oh don't apologise dear. Anyway – it's nice to have a bit of company." She patted the step next to her.

"Would you like to share my lunch? I have hard boiled eggs, virginia ham sandwiches and maple-layer cake. I know rationing has stopped in England, but it can still be awkward can't it?"

Marcia looked around. Now that the black plastic bag had slumped back into the gutter people seemed to be walking past paying no attention. She slowly climbed the two steps and sat next to the old lady on the third.

The old lady put two hard boiled eggs onto Bakelite picnic plates, with a little dish of salt by the side. She cracked and removed the shell from her own, biting into the centre with yellowing teeth and gaping gums. Marcia followed suit; picked a little salt out of the silver dish sprinkling it onto her egg.

They surveyed each other in silence as they ate the eggs and the quartered sandwiches without crusts.

The old lady then took a silver handled knife and cut into a light pale cream sponge cake with syrup oozing from the centre. Marcia helped herself to a slice, it was delicious, so light and tasty. The old lady giggled as saliva and cake slipped from her garish red mouth. "Whoops-a-daisy" she said, removing a sparkling white napkin from a silver holder and dabbing the corners of her sagging mouth.

"Of course we could only watch the wedding in black and white on the television screen," she continued, "although we are getting colour photographs now in the *New York Post*. But then we do have Grace Kelly in our country, she is SO lovely. Did you see her in Fourteen Hours? Do you know honey, she's only a year older than me!"

Marcia looked at her incredulously; although so thin and old there was something quite special about her; she must have been elegant and beautiful at one time.

"Can I ask you something?" she asked.

"Fire away, honey."

"Why are you here?"

"Here? Right here, now?"

"Yes."

"Well my dear, I shall let you into a secret, I met Max in New York," she confided, one hand on Marcia's arm, "and he changed my life!"

"Oh. Really?"

"He sure did, he begged me to come over to England. So I got the 'Carolina' to the Tilbury docks and here I am!" She lifted both hands into the air dramatically.

Delving into her bag she removed a lipstick and powder compact and deftly applied more, mouthing a bright red Ooo and Aah in the mirror, powdered her nose, snapped the compact shut and dropped it into her bag.

"The Tilbury docks? But aren't they in London?"

"Oh bless you, I'm not silly, Max told me he would make me into a film star and we would be famous like Shakespeare and his leading lady. You know Shakespeare – from Stratford-upon-Avon," she enunciated. "We got married by special licence in the States," she whispered. "But then – he wasn't at the docks so I took the London & Northern line out here to Stratford." She paused and looked wistfully into the distance and then up at the clock. "He's awfully late though."

Marcia shuffled, feeling awkward, "Look – Er – I'm sure he'll be here soon," she said, lightly placing her fingers on the old lady's arm.

"Yes of course he will – Now here I am talking nineteen to the dozen, you must think I'm awfully rude so, tell me all about yourself. What are you called and who's your favourite film star?"

"Marcia, I'm called Marcia"

"Ooh – as in Marcia Rae Jones?" she asked clasping her hands together.

"Who? No, I'm Marcia Steinman. I'm from a company in the midlands, that sells retirement-homes. We're looking for a new salesperson, someone who knows how to convince people to sell their home and move into one of ours. We intend it to be kitted out with an IT centre, quiet room, restaurant and a gym."

"And a record player with all the recent Buddy Holly and Bing Crosby songs and a cinema? You must have a cinema with Pathe News and Rank Advertising and a

Coffee Bar," interrupted the old lady, looking delighted.

Marcia looked confused.

"Oh come honey, I don't want to hear about work. A pretty girl like you must have a beau, maybe even a husband?" she nudged Marcia gently.

Marcia hesitated, "No, not at the moment, I've just been trying to get somewhere."

"And me darling! We're like two peas in a pod, trying to get somewhere. Just like Dorothy and the Tin Man and of course that ol' lion an' tufty scarecrow. We could be sisters. Why honey, I bet you're the same age as me," she declared. With the back of her hand, she lightly tucked a strand of hair behind Marcia's ear with cold fingers, careful not to touch her with her long, scarlet, horned nails.

Marcia looked around her feeling increasingly concerned. "Look, shouldn't you be in a home or something. What's your name? I think we ought to get you somewhere, you're freezing."

"No Marcia Steinman," she answered after a pause and in a determined voice, as she drew her hand back. "I expect Max will be here shortly, I don't want to miss him now do I? After all I've been waiting a long time," she said, looking up at the clock again.

"If he's not here when I leave work tonight, will you come with me? I feel responsible – somehow."

"Oh shoo you, I'm quite capable of looking myself, you hurry along."

"Oh, all right. Bye then. What did you say your name was?"

"Irene. Irene Van-Housen Ledbetter..."

Later that afternoon, Justin looked across at Marcia running his fingers through his hair.

"What's up Marcia? I thought we were looking for someone who could talk these old dears into parting with their money. You've picked some social worker who says 'we have to keep the clients happy, safe and warm putting their interests first,' he mimicked. "What's going on? You've been out of it since lunch time! Did you bang your head as well, when you fell over?"

"It's just, maybe we should think outside the box Justin. After all, they must feel so lost and lonely."

"Well you've had a sudden change of heart, what's all this with the old films and music? You've never mentioned that before. Quite frankly Marcia, I'm lost."

"What if they live forever though Justin? We'd want them to be happy."

"Get real Marcia, no one lives for ever," he sighed.

As soon as they finished work, Marcia left the office and ran towards the clock tower. Throwing her coat over her shoulder she looked up – the rain was on its way, possibly a heavy downfall. Across the road she saw police removing barriers and clearing up the final bits of rubbish from the ripped bin liner. At the base of the clock tower she looked around. The policemen drifted off.

But where was she, where was Irene?

She saw a single black glove lying on the second step under a large stone, fingers stretched towards her. Underneath she found a folded piece of pale azure writing paper. As she opened it and read the scrawling blue writing, tears began to fall down her cheeks onto the paper mingling with the falling rain.

"Dearest Marcia

Max came for me. I knew he would.
  I hope your job works out for you, I know we all have to contribute to get the countries back into shape, but secretly I hope and pray you find your beau and learn to love again like I have.
  Max says it won't take long to get where we're going and it will be a lovely place where we'll both be very rich and live happily ever after.
  By the way, I loved your Chanel outfit.
  Lovely to meet you darling. I'll see you in my dreams.

  Goodnight
  Irene."

THE CAVALIER

"Steady, left a bit, back a bit."

The man in black cap and sweater, sporting the name of the Worcester Regiment, guides the driver of the red Volvo hatchback into a spot between the Mondeo Estate 'with trailer' and new caravan swift 'with awning'.

He sprints gallantly back to his spot by the opened farm gate and directs the next car to a place on the field by the brook, a suitable distance from the portaloo.

Some of the regiment have been there a couple of hours already, dogs sniffing the tent posts and children swaying towards one another looking for an opening to start a conversation.

The battle will start at 11 o'clock the next morning. Families have an afternoon to pitch tent, set up the calor gas stoves, air the costumes and visit the pub for ale, pie and chips.

At 10.50am, the paying audience prepare for the re-enactment of the 1645 battle between Roundheads and Cavaliers. They place their deckchairs and fold-up fishing stools behind the blue plastic ribbon on the lawn. The defined battle ground is within the great Castle Walls. The visitors sit their children in front on rugs, where they demand ice creams and lollies before the show begins.

Once this majestic ruined castle took its shape in boulders and rounded turrets reaching to the blue sky. The entrance to dining and stately guest rooms still discernable from arched apex and key-stone.

To the front (beyond the perimeter of the make-shift stage) the stables stand on cobbled foundations. The thick brown timber frame held together by hand forged nails once supporting a plaster of hair, lime and sand and the old oak doors open wide to reveal a tea-room with cream teas and jam.

The loudspeaker emits a high pitched tone. An important person in green felt jacket and brown breeches leaps forth to give instructions; "Check the cables, incorrect frequency," he commands a younger fellow in similar apparel. More to-ing and fro-ing results in a change of leads and pleasant buzz from one of the speakers, strategically placed at the far end of the battle pitch.

Then in stride four Cavaliers (hooray). Straining forward two by two, hauling thick ropes over their shoulders, at the end of which is a squat grey cannon. They are followed by their ten compatriots in red jackets, large black boots; their pikes held aloft as they tip their black hats and jaunty feathers to the audience.

They take the far end.

Now follow the Roundheads. More sombre in

their jackets and breeches, helmets covering their short hair and breastplates swelling their chests. They lift their muskets high as they head their team, pulling their cannon to the nearer side of the allotted ground.

Will the battle begin?

No. First a ten minute explanation by Oliver Cromwell, as we go back in time over the centuries to the English Civil War.

"The forthcoming battle is from the 17th Century. Charles the first and his royalist supporters claimed absolute power, but ….," the commentator drones on. The army fidgets, adrenaline already at play.

At the castle entrance by the tiltyard, the ticket collector sits, checking the entrance tickets of the latecomers, shushing them, pointing to an empty space to spread their picnic rugs and coats. The children climb over the fallen sandstone walls.

Back in time. The tiltyard stood above the great earthen dam, holding back the lake, filled with colourful, sharp teethed pikes and carp. The jousting tournaments were watched from the erected wooden galleries, or from the safety of Mortimer's Tower. The Knights fighting for the favours of the fluttering, watching ladies.

Queen Elizabeth visits, with a magnificent entourage. Her eyes, on one person only in the tournament. And when her Lord Dudley wins, he takes her hand and leads her to a place at the head of his Jacobean oak table in the Great Hall. Here she is served fresh fish and oven baked bread, game from the surrounding forests with rich red wine and mead in silver goblets poured from earthenware jugs.

Bang! The cannon explodes. Great gulfs of smoke erupting from its mouth. The Cavalier stands back, his gunpowder plunger held awkwardly at his side.

Bang! The Roundheads retort from the far side of the pitch, muskets placed upright to the side (health and safety). The dogs bark and the smaller children start to cry.

And the crows fly from their battlements across the farmlands into the safety of the neighbouring woods where sheep and oxen graze, tended by villagers working 'til sunset before returning over fallows and fields, to their waiting wives and barefoot children and meal of gruel.

The Cavaliers lift their pikes aloft.

"We aim for the face or upper arm, as the rest of the body is protected," we are informed.

They dance with their pikes.

"Then we follow with the sword (seen here to the right of the body)."

The Roundheads remain in their places while the cavaliers demonstrate, from a safe distance. The opposing side repeats the actions, so we all know how to do it.

The toilets are visited frequently. The sign points to the building behind the herb garden, by Lancaster's Tower.

Purple and green lavenders are used to scent the bed linen and rid the linen closets of moths. Sage and comfrey, lifting their healing bodies to the sun are used as spices or in herbal teas.

They bask in the soft touch of the honey bees. And the thyme is crushed to a pulp to poultice festering wounds.

A cheer goes up. Hooray. The Roundheads, now down on one knee aim, fire and – 'crack'. Off go the muskets, again. Two Cavaliers are carried off on stretchers to their fluttering, plump, aproned and capped womenfolk, acting their part in this play.

The drums roll and the buglers play.

'Crack.' Three Roundheads go down with one shot. Amazing. One team has won and they all wipe their sweaty heads with their greying sleeves. Those still alive (and those fully recovered from their mortal wounds) march off the arena to the cheers of the crowd and the safety of their cars and tents outside the castle walls.

The Castle looks still further back in time. Through the vertical slits in the walls, the soldiers hold on to their lives as they loop their arrows onto the advancing armies approaching from the north at the far end of the great moat. The vats of boiling oil are balanced in place high above the battlements, in case the attackers manage to cross the moat. The drawbridge crashes down and the King Henry's Army push through the barriers, steel armour glinting in the setting sun, their white tunics emboldened with the fighting red lion. They swipe off hands and ears in the turmoil as they begin their attack on the Barons who dared to stand for their rights and suggest a country ruled in another, fairer way.

THE DINNER LADY

Geoffrey had done well for himself. Only last night his friends at the golf club had raised their glasses, patted him on the back and toasted him—

"Whoa, who's the lucky guy then?"

He, Geoffrey Manson, was the lucky guy. Jean had agreed to marry him.

They had been courting for eighteen months. Courting was an old fashioned word, but it suited them because that's what it had been-courting. They had been out together once a week over the last eighteen months; to the pictures, for a drink or a nice meal in a restaurant.

But now – Geoffrey didn't want to be on his own anymore. He needed someone to share his life with, someone to accompany him to golf dos and well, other things.

In six weeks time they would be man and wife.

Jean put the phone down,

"Mum," her daughter had argued, "I think you should wait a little longer, he's a bit pompous and Jake and I don't relate to him very well. Besides – there will be plenty to do when bump arrives."

It wasn't fair. Ok – she was going to be a grandma soon and she wanted to help out with the baby. But

Natalie had her own life now and it was so lonely in this little bungalow at times.

She had been widowed for seven years and it had been hard work. Jean had managed to keep going but it would be such a relief to have someone to look after HER for a change, someone to make decisions and help her pay the bills and do stuff online and all the other things which she found difficult.

She put the kettle on – 5 o'clock, time for a nice cuppa and a biscuit. School closed at 3.30, after the dinner ladies had cleared up the kitchens and had their dinners. She liked being a 'dinner lady' not a catering assistant as some of the parents called them. A dinner lady, and they had such a laugh, her and the other 'girls'.

Geoffrey arranged another round with Mike before they left the club. Still plenty of late afternoon sun for a good view over the fairway. Perhaps they could carry on playing a little later into the evening next week, then have a drink?

Mike had retired from work now, but he had grandchildren by the dozen. He managed to find time to play golf between babysitting and school concerts.

Geoffrey was fortunate, he didn't have children. He had been married once before but she had had an affair, Sarah, the little tart. Jeannie wasn't like that, she was trustworthy and went to church. He doubted that there would be much competition either. It used to drive him mad with Sarah, he knew all the other men were looking at her.

Geoffrey downed his orange juice and pulled in his stomach. He liked to watch his weight and at six foot two and 55 years old, he still looked the part. He lifted his golf bag, putting his other arm across Mike's shoulder as they left, "See you next week mate," Geoff said as they walked through the swing doors and he focused on his large shiny black Audi in the car park.

Natalie lifted the babygro off the hanger and turned it around looking at the price tag. She stroked and patted her six month bump affectionately.

"It's not that we don't like him mum, it's just that he doesn't seem that easy going. You're the friendly type, look how many friends you have at church and at school. The teachers, dinner ladies and children – they all love you. Why do you need to marry him, can't you just live with him? It's not as if there are many fireworks between you both as far as I can see!"

"Nattie, I want a man for myself. It's been seven years since your Dad died. It's lovely having you and Jake nearby but it's time I moved on. Geoffrey's a good man and I've always found it hard to make decisions on my own and deal with money and everything. I don't see why I have to defend myself all the time. Besides, it gets lonely at night time."

"Shag him then Mum. You should do that first in any case you know, you might not be compatible."

"Nattie! Its not just about sex – although I must admit I am looking forward to – you know. Its about companionship too, someone there for me."

"Seriously Mum, have you ever wondered why he

hasn't wanted to stop the night or anything? I mean come on, this is the Twenty First Century."

"He respects my faith love, although heaven knows his willpower must be stronger than mine," Jean admitted ruefully, as she gently took the babygros off her daughter to pay for them at the counter. "Let's have a coffee and a cake before you go back."

"Mum, your tummy is as big as mine! I'll have soup and a salad. You go ahead, does Geoffrey like small and plump?"

Jean did not reply.

Jean looked around her kitchen as she wiped her floured hands on her apron. Her bungalow had sold as soon as the for-sale sign went up. The estate agent had negotiated the white goods in the purchase price. A single parent was buying it, that was nice.

She wouldn't need to take a lot of stuff to Geoffrey's four bedroomed detached house. The plan was; she would pay off his remaining mortgage once her sale had completed and he would then put his house into joint names.

He had made his money in IT, so clever, setting up all those systems. Jean felt a little overwhelmed, a school dinner lady marrying an IT consultant, wasn't she the lucky one!

Jean looked at the large quiche in front of her. It had been cooling for 10 minutes. She had made quite a few things now for the party. They had decided to have a small registry office wedding, then a blessing in church followed by a party at his house (well their house now) – with close family and friends. At Geoff's suggestion, they had postponed their honeymoon for a week so that they could deal with all of the goings-on.

Jean took a slice of the quiche and popped it into her mouth, letting the pastry crumble under her tongue and savouring the tasty cheesy bacon filling. She cut the rest up, she would let it cool, then wrap each piece and put it in the freezer together with the other goodies mounting up for the evening do. You could never be too sure. She was determined they were not going to go short on her special day.

She had enjoyed cooking for her hubby Terry, she reflected. There was never a day Terry hadn't thanked and appreciated her for her efforts, patting her rump or nuzzling into her ample bosom. Jean missed being part of a family. There had only been the three of them, but they had had some lovely times and grand holidays by the sea. That's why she took the job of a dinner lady at the school when Terry died. She liked cooking and needed the money and the company. But soon she would give it all up and cook for Geoffrey, that might be nice.

She had chosen a smart cream suit and pale green blouse, cream shoes and a green clutch bag as her wedding outfit. Nattie seemed a bit moody when she had asked her if she would go and help her buy it. She had said she wouldn't take her advice so what was the point? So she had asked her friend Susan from the church to help. She had put it down to Nattie's condition. She remembered her own moods when she had been pregnant, up and down. But Terry had been so supportive. He had said they would have had a family of sixteen children if she hadn't lost so much blood. He said it hadn't mattered and continued to prove it to her almost every night, "Oh Terry, oh Terry, oh-my lo—"

Ah – well, she pulled herself together, wiping a tear from her eye leaving a film of flour over her cheek, that was life. She dusted her hands over her apron, mustn't get maudlin now.

"So – how's the sale going?" Mike asked when Geoff had putted into the eighth.

"Fine, it's all in the hands of the estate agent and solicitor now. We expect the exchange to go ahead during the honeymoon week. She's signed all the paperwork and we've asked for completion two weeks later when we get back from Scotland. We're only going for a week," he added. "Then I've booked the removal company to do the rest, no need for Jeannie to worry about anything."

Geoffrey swung his golf bag up on his shoulder and he and Mike moved onto the ninth hole. Geoffrey knew his game had been steadily getting worse over the last few weeks, a temporary blip, probably a few things on his mind what with the move and now the wedding only a week away. He usually managed to beat Mike but he hadn't focused well on the sixth and ninth hole which had cost him. He had also played two eights on a three and four!

Geoffrey felt angry, he'd had words with Jeannie

about her weight. She didn't seem to take much notice, but he didn't like overweight women and she seemed to be getting fatter. His wife had been tall and slim. He couldn't feel proud of Jean; she was pretty enough but by no means 'a looker' and he wouldn't be happy if she continued to take no notice of him, after they were married.

He had been to the doctor's himself recently and aired his other concern over his little problem. The doctor had said it would all be back to normal again once the waiting was over and he was a married man, so he should stop worrying about it.

He put his arm over Mike's shoulder, "Give me a break, mate!" he joked. Mike was a really nice guy.

*

It had been a great day Jean reflected as she closed the door on the last of the guests and fell into the plush cream leather sofa in the lounge with a heavy sigh. The wedding went smoothly, pictures for the album but no speeches – people hadn't known them well enough as a couple to make speeches.

All the dinner ladies had helped with the party food in the evening which had gone down a treat and everyone had seemed to enjoy the party; throwing back the drinks and hugging each other warmly as they sang and kicked off their shoes.

The 'girls' had all danced to 'Kiss me, honey, honey, kiss me,' miming Shirley Bassey's movements, what a laugh. Then the Rolling Stones – 'Brown Sugar you make me feel so good' – Jean smiled and hummed the tune.

The leader from the prayer group had got drunk on the Champers and walked around the room quoting from the Bible and blessing them all profusely. Geoffrey had phoned up for a taxi to take him home. She had had to explain to a somewhat shocked Geoffrey that they weren't all saints, all the time.

Nattie looked terrific, still graceful in her black trousers and beige maternity top. She had whispered, "As long as you're happy Mum," in her ear. Didn't they all smile as Jean passed the black and white scan of the little curled up foetus around all her friends and they had all tried to guess if it was a boy or girl. Nattie was getting a lot of care from her midwife, she would be fine, just fine. Only a few weeks to go and Jake had attended to her all evening fetching and carrying – just like—.

Anyway, she had met Geoff's sister and her family. They hadn't seemed very friendly, they had kept their bottles of wine to themselves. Appellation Controlle and Rioja or something. But then, families took a while to get to know one another. And his golfing friends seemed nice.

She pulled herself up from the sofa and walked over to Geoffrey in the kitchen. He had his back to her and was washing up at the double sink, rinsing each glass under the hot tap and lifting it to the light checking for a sparkling finish.

A little nervously, she wrapped her arms around his waist and kissed his neck.

"Let's leave the clearing up until the morning," she suggested, rubbing her hips against him.

"You go on up, Jeannie, I'll just clear away the left overs and put the plates into the dishwasher," he said disentangling her arms. "I don't like to leave dirty dishes lying around."

In the morning Geoffrey turned towards her and lay on his side. "Jeannie, I would like to wait until our honeymoon to make this moment really special," he announced, without touching her.

Jean hid her face in the pillow as she felt the disappointment wash over her.

*

They stopped for an early dinner on the journey up, arriving in the evening before it was dark. They had been given the honeymoon suite overlooking the lake. Geoffrey had chosen Scotland and this hotel in Perthshire was ideal, it had its own par 72 golf course.

In fact, as soon as they got into their bedroom, he looked out of the window. The first hole was beyond the lake, he would use a Wood from a tee and maybe get 200 yards.

Using his binoculars to look down the fairway he could still just see the flag for the second in the bunker, fantastic! He could use his sand wedge, to hit the green. Exciting.

Jeannie fumbled for the lightswitch and disappeared into the luxurious bathroom and opened her handbag. She sat on the toilet and crammed the chocolate bar into her mouth.

She went back into the bedroom and collected her toilet bag and filled the bath with hot soapy water using the complimentary lavender bath gel. Looking down at her stomach she felt ugly and dirty. It shouldn't be this way. Maybe tonight? He had said it was something they would appreciate in years to come and there was nothing wrong with waiting until the time was right. She would have a hot scented bath, use the hotels' lovely big white fluffy towels, then put on something nice and go downstairs with Geoffrey for the welcome cocktails. Back in their room she would put on her new long silky red nightie, in front of him – and then who knows? It was, after all, the first night of their honeymoon.

Geoffrey rolled off Jean's body. "I'm sorry, it's just that you are so fat Jean and it really doesn't turn me on. You will have to lose weight, why have you let yourself go like this for Gods sake?"

Jean drew her nightie down to her ankles and held back the sobs. She turned over to her side of the bed reaching for the bedside light. She looked down onto the rich-pile carpet on the floor by the side of the bed and noticed biscuit crumbs in the carpet as she switched off her light.

Geoffrey sighed accusingly, then reached to touch his new 'St Andrews' sweatshirt which he had carefully folded on the chair by the side of the bed. He would wear it tomorrow. He gently tucked the tissue paper in at the sides and switched off his bedside light.

Breakfast was in the vast dining room with Jacobean Oak tables covered in thick white linen table cloths and beautifully arranged autumnal flowers as centre pieces.

They had been directed to their table by a smart waiter who clicked his fingers and a hot silver coffee pot with freshly-ground coffee arrived at their table.

Jean put her handbag on the floor to the side of the chair and toyed with the white linen napkin. She didn't dare ask for a cup of tea. She restricted herself to a little fruit and the cereal with natural yoghurt.

Geoffrey had the cooked breakfast from the hot silver urns lined up against the walnut panelled wall and resisted the danish pastries and croissants placed enticingly on the side table by the entrance.

He smiled and made polite conversation with the other guests.

Jean watched the large rotary toaster turn over the bread and pop the slices out at the bottom.

Geoffrey disappeared to the back of the hotel once breakfast was over, leaving Jean to 'have some time to herself'.

Jean walked slowly back up the stairs holding the sweeping wooden banister. She looked into the faces of the people in the gold framed pictures on the way up and inclined her head as she studied their mouths, their eyes and aristocratic noses and wondered who they were.

She reached the bedroom and walked to the window and peeped out from behind the curtains.

Geoffrey was tying up the laces of his new golf shoes. She watched as he slowly straightened himself up. He was only a few inches away from his opponent; a man he had arranged a round with the evening before, immediately after their welcome cocktails in the lounge.

The window slightly open, she could almost hear them, but neither looked her way. She watched as they warmed-up. She saw how Geoffrey slowly and sensuously pulled himself up and stretched his arms above his head, bending to right and left, opening his legs and turning to twist his upper body from side to side, gently circling his feet at the ankles one way, then the other. They started to practice their swing together taking a step backwards and forwards as they moved the imaginary golf club high above their shoulders to swing it through to the front. Above to the back and through to the front, above to the back and through to the front, in time with each other.

She sat on the bed holding her bag to her breast. She had a magazine which she could read as she waited for him.

She thumbed through her magazine and put it to one side with a sigh.

She felt inside her bag and took out her lipstick. With shaking hands she opened the compact and using the mirror, applied the pink paste to her lips. She closed it and dropped it back into her bag and looked towards the window.

She opened her bag again and felt into its depth.

She slowly brought out two croissants, two

little tubs of butter and a miniature pot of jam, all wrapped together in a white napkin. She walked to the morning tea tray and took the teaspoon. Using the back of the spoon she spread the butter and jam over the croissants gently moving the folds of delicate pastry to make sure all was covered.

She licked the spoon and her fingers one at a time. Then she sank her teeth into the rich sweet pastry savouring every mouthful as the jam oozed out around her pink lips.

THE ESTATE AGENT

She stuffed the empty lager can behind the sofa, it clinked as it hit the others pushed up against the wall. She switched the television off, rushed into the kitchen and had started to fill the dishwasher by the time his key turned in the front door.

She was used to the sound of the BMW on the gravel driveway, he had an irritating way of revving up the engine just before turning off the ignition.

He had taken to 'dropping in' on his way to visit a prospective client in the area. It irritated her, she couldn't relax. He didn't phone before hand to say "I'm on my way home darling, fancy a coffee?"

Oh no, he would drop in and find fault.

"For Gods sake woman, haven't you finished yet?" he shouted from the hall as he looked through to the newly fitted kitchen with central island. "It's 11 o' clock and the house is in a mess."

("As usual" – she added under her breath.)

He picked up the post from the hall table and opened the telephone bill. Helen kept her head low. She had long ago realised that the best way to deal with him was to refrain from answering back, just keep quiet. There was no point in trying to talk or explain.

"You've been on the phone to your bloody sister again, couldn't you get her to give you a ring now and again? Why does it have to come out of my hard-earned money?" he complained as he walked into the kitchen, waving the telephone bill in her face.

"Gerard, you know Sheila hasn't been well recently. She rings me too you know, as often as I ring her! I told you her MS was developing at a worrying pace. She may have to start using a wheelchair soon and I'm very worried about her."

Too late! She had answered back, now there would be more fault-finding, he wouldn't let go of this.

"I'm not surprised you find time to gossip, after all what DO you do with yourself all day?"

("Stupid woman", Helen muttered under her breath, finishing his sentence for him.) She bent down to put the last plate into the dishwasher, throwing the mask over her face.

He put the kettle on and made himself a cup of instant coffee, but he didn't make her one.

"I'll be late home tonight, I have a meeting."

'Oh – Good,' she thought.

She heard the front door click shut. Breathing a sigh of relief, she walked through the lounge, over to the drinks cabinet to pour herself a whisky, she deserved it. She didn't often drink spirits at this time of day but he made her nervous and a whisky calmed her down. There wasn't much left, she might as well finish the bottle. The lead-crystal glass would be nice and a few ice cubes. She hid the empty bottle behind the curtain. She would take it outside and put it in the plastic shopping bag in the corner of the shed. Or stuff it in an empty cereal box and hide it deep in the dustbin later – when she wasn't so tired.

She looked out of the large bay window into the driveway of the identical five bedroomed, two reception roomed house opposite. It would have exactly the same en-suite attached to the master bedroom and two extra bathrooms. Mock Georgian double glazed windows throughout. As would the house next door to that and the one next door to that… However, they had been cleverly built at a slight angle to one another in the cul-de-sac so that they were not overlooked. You could stay safely indoors without being seen. Feeling – well – isolated.

Helen slumped down on the sofa glass in hand and flicked the television on, barely registering the morning quiz show. Two years ago when they had first moved in, she would have answered some of the questions but now she didn't bother. It was a noise in the background to break up the silence.

Business was going well for Gerard Kline. He had been lucky enough to find a growing suburb with a good catchment area and there were no other estate agents near by. Some of his customers felt they would reach a wider audience of buyers in the town centre. But he managed to persuade them that prospective buyers would look in this newer, smarter area of Gloucestershire.

Peoples' homes were their castles. After all a

house represented who you were in life and what you had achieved.

He had a tactic of telling his customers he was able to sell their property for more than he knew he would get for it. Then he would advertise; glamourising the property, showing shots of the back garden taken with an enlarging lens. Once they had an interested buyer who naturally offered less than the asking price, he would encourage the seller to drop the price to get the sale. By this time the seller had another property in mind, so negotiated less on their own purchase. Worked every time.

He thought about his own property – they had moved there when Louisa left home; it was smart, it was clean, it was tidy. Louisa's room was always there for her. His Louisa, his daughter, the apple of his eye. She was a bright, pretty young thing, like Helen had been, once. She was twenty and enjoying her second year at university. He hoped she would stay to the end and not get pregnant like her mother. He didn't think much of her choice of subject; Environmental Science. She wouldn't go on about global warming when she left home and got married. Women were strange creatures, thank God he didn't have the time to think about these things.

He so often had to work after 5pm to interview prospective clients as both partners worked in full time jobs these days. But he didn't tonight, so he would stop off and have a couple of pints on his way home, he deserved it. He had got into the habit of stopping for a couple at the pub – if he didn't have to work late. At least he could find someone to talk to at the bar.

He had thought that by giving up her 'little job' at the day centre Helen would have found more time for him, he mused. But she hadn't. She always seemed to be asleep on the sofa in the evening. Then when he looked for her in the king size bed at night, she would be in the lounge, the television droning away. Last night he had gone downstairs to find her. She had jumped when he came into the room, burying her hands under the throw. If she chose to sleep downstairs instead of in the marital bed then that was her problem.

Helen heard Gerard coming down the stairs this time, she had nearly been caught out last night.

She buried the empty lager cans under the throw and feigned sleep.

He walked in and looked at her, coughed and sniffed wiping his nose on his dressing gown sleeve. He scratched his arse, looking at her again, then went back up to bed.

Revolting pig.

At 4am, she picked up her mobile phone from the coffee table and texted Sheila.

'How've u bin tday pet x?'

'T'day? Is that ystdy or the 4hrs of tday?'

'Both.'

'Fell over again on way 2 hosptl, more tests t,mrw. Can u cum up?'

'Will try, but still probs leaving house – nerves bad, get frite-nd.'

'Luv u, wish I cud help.'

'U do. Always u do, L U 2.'

"Where are you and your husband thinking of moving to Mrs Larkin? Have you somewhere in mind? I have quite a few properties on my books at the moment and I am sure if you sell with me and buy with me we can come to some sort of a deal."

"Thank you Mr Kline, but we want to take our time with this decision. I would like to move back into the town, it's so sterile here don't you think? One can get so lonely."

"On the contrary, Foxwood Grove is a well established area. They've set up local shops and bus routes over the last two years. In fact my wife and I live just across the road," he said pointing to the opposite driveway. "So you have picked the right person, I know these houses like the back of my hand. Lovely coffee by the way Mrs Larkin, you can't beat freshly brewed."

Helen was emptying the shopping out onto the kitchen worktop just as Gerard's car entered the drive. The supermarket delivered straight to the house, which helped as she was probably over the limit already. Besides, she seemed unable to cope in crowded supermarkets these days.

She quickly hid three of the six bottles of wine in the cupboard under the sink with the cleaning fluids.

This had always proved to be a good hiding place as Gerard never dreamed of looking in the cleaning cupboard. Why would he? He wouldn't know a bleach from a polish.

He seemed to be in a better frame of mind, he hadn't slammed the front door and had called out her name as he entered the house.

"Good news. I think I've clinched the deal on number 7, directly opposite." He said as he pointed in the direction of the end of the drive.

"You'll never guess! I can probably get four hundred grand on that, which means our place has gone up by a hundred grand, in two years Helen!"

Helen lifted her face from the supermarket bags and boxes.

"That's good Gerard. Perhaps we could sell and move to the North to be nearer my sister?"

"You must be joking, woman, we're sitting on a gold mine here. We'll have a decent meal and a couple of bottles of wine to celebrate after I get home tonight."

Helen toyed with her food, moving the steak around her plate and accepted another glass of wine. The second bottle had been carefully opened by Gerard just as they had started to eat, so it could breathe. Gerard put his knife and fork down and belched loudly. "Must be the excitement of the housing deals I've done recently," he said holding his stomach.

(What a paunch, he's disgusting, thought Helen.)

"By the way Gerard; don't drink too much. Louisa

phoned earlier, she may be coming home tonight for a half term break. Last minute as always, bless her. She'll need picking up from the station – if she decides to come."

"What! Why didn't you tell me earlier? Oh well its not far I suppose. The police don't patrol this area, they stay around the council estate, that's where the troublemakers live Helen, mark my word. In the centre of town, not places like this."

Helen started clearing away as the phone rang. Seeing Louisa's mobile number she put it on loudspeaker.

"Hi Mummy, can you or Daddy come and get me?" Louisa sang out.

Helen looked at Gerard. "Gerard I think it's best to tell her to get a taxi and we'll pay the driver when she gets here," she whispered.

Gerard snatched the phone out of the holder.

"I'm on my way darling," he said, talking loudly into the mouthpiece, "wait outside the station entrance for me."

Helen began pacing the lounge floor, they should have been back within twenty minutes, it was now an hour later and no sign of them. She made another cup of coffee and looked apprehensively towards the garage. Should she go and look for them? She hadn't driven for six months.

Two cars entered the drive.

Louisa ran into the house and dropped her rucksack on the floor.

"Mummy!" She burst into tears as a sheepish Gerard came through the front door, closely followed by two police officers. Both young, one male and one female.

"Mrs Kline? I'm afraid your husband has been cautioned. He's breathalysed well over the limit, so we'll have to take him with us into custody. We found him urinating against a tree in front of the station too."

Helen put her hand to her face, "Oh Gerard, how could you, I *did* warn you."

Gerard snarled quietly, "Shut up stupid woman."

Turning to the policewoman, he said in his best salesman's voice, "I'm sure there must be some mistake, Constable."

He gestured to the police to sit down as he hospitably pulled the sofa forward – nearer the fire.

There was a loud clatter as the room filled with rolling, empty lager cans emerging from behind the sofa. They trickled out warm, sickly smelling dregs, from their bent and punctured bodies.

The FOR SALE sign went up two weeks later in Foxwood Grove.

'Gerard Kline Real Estates.'

Helen stood by the side of the Clio and looked over at the sign. She opened the passenger door of the car and Louisa climbed in.

"I'll run you back to the station, and see you at Christmas."

"Ok." Louisa sadly handed her mother her

rucksack. "Mummy, I never knew Daddy drank so much!"

"It came as a shock to me too. The police helped me find empty whisky bottles hidden behind curtains and extra wine bottles under the sink!"

"Can we get him help, can the doctor do anything?"

"I don't know, sweetheart, he seems to be in denial saying he knows nothing about it. He says he never has more than a couple of beers a day. But the day he was breathalysed he was well over the limit!"

"What will you do now?" Louisa asked, still concerned.

"First and foremost, I'm going to see Auntie Sheila for a couple of weeks. I've missed her and we have so much to talk about. Then I might do a college course again. Who knows, pick-up my languages where I left off years and years ago. They are just ideas now, but it will be something to focus on to help me get through the next few months."

"Oh Mummy, I am sorry. Will Daddy lose his job?"

"More than likely. The problem is – he needs the car to visit properties and clients."

Helen shut the passenger door and walked to the back of the car. She unlocked the boot and swung the rucksack into the back, it chinked as it hit half a dozen black bin bags removed from the shed. She would drive round to the tip after she had dropped Louisa off at the station. Might as well get rid of the rest of the evidence now, Gerard would have enough to cope with.

Shutting the boot, she looked across the road. With a grin on her face, she waved cheerily at Mrs Larkin peering out from behind her curtain at the 'For Sale' sign in Gerard and Helen's front garden.

She paused, took a deep relaxing breath and contentedly returned to the driving seat. Time for her to get on with her own life now.

THE HOUSE CLEARANCE

Outside, the February sky was beginning to darken and the rain drew dashes against the window, blurring the images as she looked down on the traffic and passers by, two floors below. The afternoon was dragging by for Sinead and she knew she needed to concentrate on her students if they were to pass the latest Art and Design assignment.

She took a deep breath lifting her red hair to massage the ache at the back of her neck and stretch her arms.

They say it takes a couple of years to get over the death of a close relative, she reflected as she took a last look at the grey sky outside. Had they been close? Once? Ever? All that remained of her father were a few rare but precious memories of her childhood. Once he had taken a day off work to take the family out for a picnic. He had played hide and seek with her and her elder brother, swooping her up into the sky when he found her. Another time they had had a beach holiday in County Wicklow; collecting crabs, building sandcastles and swimming, but they had had to leave suddenly, so he could go back to work, to an auction, so he said. He didn't have a steady job, but managed to bring in an income from his many trips away. Her mother always forgave him saying she had married him knowing he was a bit of a devil, with the luck of the Irish.

Her brother had left home after he finished university and now lived in England. Her mother had died, when she herself had just started university. Then there had just been her and him, with little left to say to each other, his spark had left him. And now her little maisonette in Belfast, which she had managed to get two years ago on a scraped together mortgage, was full of him and his precious antiques and paintings which her mother had hated and hidden away in cupboards. They were itemised on her computer and priced for insurance at today's market value. But she hadn't got around to selling them, so they were still packed in bubble wrap and cardboard boxes. The paintings were propped against every available wall, awaiting 'multiple layering' and 'optical colour mix' before selling.

She sighed and turned back to the class trying to focus on the next student, waiting with work samples and opened portfolio. She found her thoughts drifting to the hot scented bath and glass of wine she would have at the end of the day.

Sinead clutched her bag full of reports to her chest and let herself in through her front door. She had the upstairs apartment, accessed through the side of the block of four.

She started to climb the flight of stairs to the kitchen-diner at the top. She could see a light on through the slightly opened door at the top of the stairs.

She hadn't left the light on when she had left that morning – no, she was sure she hadn't.

She turned back to look at the closed front door. She felt sure she had double-locked it this morning. Yes she always did, checking it religiously.

A dreadful feeling of foreboding rooted her to the spot half way up the stairs, should she call for help? Maybe call Patrick, her boyfriend? She tentatively inched her way upwards, legs shaking with every step.

She brushed past her own attempts at oil paintings, fixed to the stairwell by picture hooks. Seaviews stretching across the northern shores, with kittiwakes and gulls. Ceilidh gatherings – where folk merged into each other, colours of saffron and green blending with dancing feet and flowing hair. Settling them quietly into place, she held her breath, her back against the wall.

She reached the top step and the kitchen door. What if someone had broken in and was still in the kitchen, she thought – with a knife? Oh God!

She thought about her father's antiques, his 'stuff' as she called it, piled around the floor. She should have sold it, but he was insistent on photographing every item and getting a good valuation – almost right until the day he died. He told her to wait until the time was right – but she had no idea when 'the right time' would be, so she had done nothing. He said she would be able to get a good price, "when the time comes, trust me, darlin'!"

"This is quality," he had boasted; tenderly handling the French Mantel Clock or Worcester Urn.

Still clutching her workload under one arm, Sinead slowly pushed the door to the kitchen. Gasping she held her hand to her throat.

The room was empty!

The original Ikea kitchen she had painstakingly fitted, when she first moved in, was still intact; no marks on the cupboards or worktops. The modern designer clock on the wall still in place. The food processor and microwave secure on the worktop. Her laptop on the desk in the corner. All still there.

But her father's boxes of antiques – normally taking up all her floor space – and his watercolours stacked together around the walls, all of them gone. Disappeared!

Sinead tentatively put her workload down on the dining table. What should she do?

She took a bread-knife from the kitchen drawer and the hammer from under the sink. Fingers trembling she placed them at hand and lifted the phone dialling 999, somehow managing to recount the sequence of events from this morning – until now, to the gently spoken policewoman at the other end of the phone.

She should really call Patrick, she thought as she replaced the receiver, or a friend to come and sit with her, until the Gardai arrived.

She walked around the kitchen. Touching the now clear shiny worktops and fingering the dials on the microwave, revelling at the space in the room and smart black and white tiles exposed on the floor.

There again, maybe she wouldn't phone a friend,

she thought as she caressed the zany wallclock… her shoulders gently relaxing back into place.

She smiled inwardly, maybe champagne? When the Gardai left, of course. She put a bottle in the fridge to chill and opened the cupboard, lifting out one clear glass flute from a set of four.

"Cheers Dad, good on you."

THE NEST

Rachel knocked on her neighbour's front door.

"Hi. Just to let you know, I'm having a few roof tiles replaced today. The roofer may have to use your drive for his ladders. Is that ok?"

Her neighbour sniffed disapprovingly. Stretching her neck outside her small red-brick porch, she looked up and down the road before she replied.

"How long will he take?"

"I don't know, sorry," Rachel said. "He will be here at nine. But I might get him to look at the guttering too. So it could be until lunchtime." Rachel added apologetically, as she fiddled with her long brown hair. She took an elastic hair-band from her pocket and tying it into an efficient ponytail, flicked it behind her shoulders.

Her neighbour sniffed again, folded her arms over her chest and stepped out of the porch onto her front drive to look up at the guttering running over her adjoining terraced property.

"I don't want any of that black plastic stuff." She went inside and shut her door.

"And would you like to pay for your share," Rachel muttered to the closed door. She looked down at her feet. She curled her toes up inside her sneakers and walked across the drive to her own front door.

She had taken to dropping notes in whenever possible, written on the back of a flyer or used envelope, rather than confronting the old crosspatch;

'The window cleaner called, I told him you weren't in and asked him to call back later.' Or, 'The TV installation company are coming today. They are installing cable for me and will be digging a channel under my front drive.'

She had been brought up to be polite and show a little respect. Rachel knew what would be happening now. Her neighbour would be phoning her friend from the next street. Every now and then they stood at the end of the row of terrace houses, arms folded across their buxom chests, grey heads shaking, cheeks puffed out and mouths pursed as they looked down the row of twelve houses disapprovingly.

Built over 150 years ago, the attractive row of Welsh red-bricked terraced houses, had sustained many alterations over the years. Windows changed from sash to leaded were again changed to white PVC. Chimneys, which once released soft peaty smells, had pepper-pots and aerials flagging their turreted tops. Front gardens, with little white gates to the roadside, were now brick paved or tarmacked for off road parking. Back gardens, once yards with washing lines, possers and mangles, were fenced off – dividing property from neighbourly conversations. The shared toilets at the bottom of the yard, had been removed or were now used as storage spaces for bar-b-ques and garden tools. The alleyway along the back of the houses, once frequented by the night-soil man, were disused and overgrown with nettles and weeds.

Rachel and the boys had moved into the little two bed roomed house a year ago, following her separation from Andrew. Downsizing and having no mortgage had seemed a good idea, until she was able to get herself on her feet again. She could manage on her maintenance payments for the boys and do the place up in the meantime.

At first she had tried to be friendly: "Hello", she said over the broken fence at the back, "my name's Rachel – aren't these sweet little houses. There's a lot to do to put things straight though – it's a good job I like DIY. Hope we're not too noisy for you."

"These walls are only one brick thick you know," her neighbour had replied before scuttling back to her own back door.

She had tentatively asked her neighbour to go halves with her on the fencing. "It's your fence," her neighbour had sniffed in reply. "Mine's the end one, mine's a semi really, she explained. So it's your problem not mine."

Rachel had given up trying to be friendly, she accepted that for reasons of her own, her neighbour had decided not to like her. But she wasn't going to apologise or take the blame for her neighbour's ignorant attitude. Oh no. She was made of tougher stuff than that, she hoped.

The children had caused her a problem at first. Her neighbour had banged on the wall every time little Tony had cried, or the boys had been arguing or playing, as boys will. So she had put up an extra layer of plasterboard on the adjoining wall followed by some very thick lining paper, which she had painted over in a nice beige colour. Now at least the noise between the houses was muffled. She managed most of the maintenance and improvements herself; painting, decorating, removing and replacing rotten floorboards. Outside, at the front, she had tidied the lovely pink climbing rose adjoining the house to her right and the honeysuckle to her left. She tried to retain as much of the original character as possible.

Rachel busied herself, no time to worry today. The twins were more settled now they were at nursery school three days a week and she could get on making her house into a cosy little nest for them all. She collected her vegetable wastes together, chopped them up and put them into the compost bucket in the yard, firmly securing the lid down with two bricks on top. Ready for using as compost on her flower tubs, in a few months time.

She washed the plastic milk bottles out and put them outside in the recycling box together with newspapers. She wiped the stainless steel sink thoroughly with disinfectant. She didn't want her boys to catch any germs.

She looked out from her kitchen window onto the compact area at the back, now awash with small borders of daffodils, primroses and tulips. She had repaired the back fence herself with fencing panels. The washing was drying nicely on the short length of line attached from the back wall to a steel washing pole, concreted securely in the ground.

It was strange how the toilet was blocked though.

She had a downstairs bathroom; most of the bathrooms were downstairs in these older houses. It was positioned at the back of the house, where the coal house had been, years ago. The terrace properties that had had an extension upstairs, with an upstairs bathroom were more expensive.

Besides, she didn't mind the fact that the bathroom was at back of the house, it somehow seemed tidier, cleaner, out of the way. But she felt alarmed. For the last few days, the toilet wastes were washing back up into the toilet. It was revolting. Her nose twitched at the thought of the smell beginning to permeate the house.

Drains-R-Us were due at any minute, this was one DIY job she didn't fancy tackling herself. The door-bell rang, bang on time. The man said he'd walk around via the back-passageway, if she could open the gate.

"What do you puts down ty bach? Nappies and the like?"

"No, the boys don't use them anymore. They're three now and at nursery school. I bag all bulky items up and put them in the general waste bin. I never wash paint down the toilet, I take the residues to the tip. I've tried a Coopers plunger on the blockage, but it doesn't work either."

"Can I be taking a look down the manhole cover outside, annwyl?"

"Of course."

He unhooked the cover and peered inside, crouching down low and shining his torch along the large waste pipe.

"Aah now see there – your drain joins up with her's next door, down the line there see," he said. "So whatever goes down 'er ty bach – goes down yours too. That's problem number one. But – see them there droppings? Them's rats! That's problem number two for you."

"Rats? But I don't leave any food around." Rachel stood motionless, her fingers stretched, her body rigid and her blue-grey eyes rounded and shocked. She thought of her meticulous disposal of any waste materials. She thought of her cupboards with tins and sealed packages, her fridge with fresh fruit and vegetables, her freezer perfectly stocked with home-made, wholesome food.

"Gets everywhere they do. Not your fault. We can bung some poison down and then they either dies an' we can collect the bodies, or they goes elsewhere most times. Very clean little varmins. Clever little critters you know, often seems to know when we coming and will disappear before we gets there," he said admiringly. "Back to that blockage. Now that's your number one problem. The best way to stop that is to separate your drains."

"Oh dear, is that a big job?"

"I should have a word with her next door and see

if you can work it out between you. Get back to us when you can and we'll sort it from there. I'll give you a fair price, don't you worry."

Rachel knocked tentatively on her neighbour's door. She could see her peeking out from behind her curtain, but she didn't come to the door. She tried again. She was ignored.

Rachel phoned Drains-R-Us the next day and said, (her voice a little high-pitched and nervous). "I'll have the work done. But I'll have to foot the bill myself as my neighbour's ignoring me again. I know from experience she'll swear its nothing to do with her."

"That's OK annwyl, we'll do a deal. Cash, cheaper and easier, that way."

True to their word Drains-R-Us arrived the following day, promptly at 8am. Plastic rods, hoists, buckets, waste outlets, discharge pipes, soil outlets on the van. Two heavy booted men disappeared round to the back yard.

There was no need for the note posted through her neighbour's door this time, it was embarrassingly obvious. The whole row of houses could see what was happening if they peered over the fences at the back or out of the door at the front.

The toilet came out and was placed ceremoniously on the back yard. The manhole cover came up. The two men drilled into the concrete and pulled, manoeuvred, hammered and scraped.

They put new, separate, sewage pipes down. They poured in the concrete.

They were there when her friend Megan, along with her own two little girls, collected and took the children to nursery school. They were still there at 12 noon when Rachel collected all four for lunch and at 3.30 when Megan brought them home at the end of the day.

At 6pm the men knocked politely on the door and brought in empty tea mugs and biscuit plates

Rachel was shaking, Tony and Simon clung to her trembling legs.

The three of them peeked into the bathroom.

The toilet was mortared back in place, spotless.

Outside the back door, the manhole cover was replaced, a pot of tulips by the side.

The mens' tools and rods were back in the van.

The daffodils in the pots were standing upright and the yard had been swept.

She thanked them profusely and paid them cash, with a little extra.

"There you go boyos, you can crap 'til yer little hearts' content, you'll have no problems now. No need for poison", he smiled tapping his finger to his nose. He teasingly pinched the boy's little pink ears as he left.

Rachel settled down for the evening, feet-up and feeling very drowsy with a glass of gooseberry wine. Finding herself nodding off to sleep, she went upstairs and checked up on the boys. They were curled around in foetus shapes on their little bunk beds. She cleaned her teeth and settled herself in her own bed.

She didn't hear the muffled sounds from next door.

No one heard her neighbour call out, sobbing in dismay as the toilet flushed over onto her own bathroom floor, spilling faeces and urine over the carpet tiles. No one saw her dive to the airing cupboard to find dry towels to mop up the mess, pulling the towels out one after the other as the effluent, stinking waste poured out and out.

No one saw her neighbour stuff her wet fist into her mouth to stop the scream as she saw something moving at the back of the cupboard. No one saw her rigid with terror, the hairs on the back of her neck rising.

Because there before her, staring at her from amongst the warm, clean towels, at the back of the airing cupboard, was a huge brown rat, suckling its tiny naked pink family, its eyes and stillness daring her to move.

The strangled sound left her throat. She screamed a cry for help. The rat leapt at her, sinking its teeth deep into her fist, its pale blue-grey eyes never leaving her face. She cried out loudly she couldn't shake it off. She banged her fist on the wall as she tried to knock the creature away. It leapt to her throat and lashed its brown tail into her cheek and eyes as it sank its teeth deep into her flesh and red, red blood gushed forth. Rachel stirred slightly. She thought she could hear the distant screech of fighting tomcats or mating foxes. She was aware of the boys turning in their little beds. She drifted off again, thinking of the geraniums she was about to propagate tomorrow for the tubs outside. Maybe she would put the pot of tulips back over the manhole cover. They wouldn't be disturbed again.

THE NEW GIRL

Alison looked over the top of the science bench towards the teacher. She shifted her goggles onto her forehead and held her deflagrating spoon aloft.

"Please Sir, the Magnesium is spitting in the flame?"

"I'm sure you'll manage Alison," he answered as he continued to measure small amounts of chemicals, placing them in petri-dishes with tweezers. The lab-assistant passed the dishes around the class putting them next to the flasks, a safe distance from the Bunsen-burners.

Alison pouted as she replaced her goggles. They were working in pairs and she didn't like the new girl next to her. She had wanted to work with Melanie, but Mel was working with Jo. She watched the new girl, she stood out like a sore thumb. Her science overall was navy-blue and the school colours were brown for the uniform and green for science overalls and sports kit. She put the spoon on the asbestos mat and removed her goggles.

"You can do something now instead of just standing there," she said rudely to the new girl. "I'm going to wash up this equipment."

She walked to the sink where Mr Kettering was rinsing his spatula and other stuff.

"Please Sir, are we supposed to put the bottles of acid back on the benches or in the fume cupboard?"

"It's diluted, so leave it on the bench," he replied, barely looking at her.

"What are we doing next week?"

No reply, try another tactic. "Sir – I didn't understand the homework you gave us last time."

"Mmh?"

"The periodic table Sir, I might need some help after school."

"Ok Alison, I'm helping a few girls from 3B but I guess I can fit you in."

Alison smiled inwardly as she turned back to the sink to wash out her funnel and test-tubes.

Melanie was on break duty, which meant she sold milk, fruit juice and biscuits. She could sneak some biscuits from the boxes into her satchel to give to her friends for lights out. It wasn't really stealing, she reasoned, because she didn't take any of the money and she didn't eat any of the biscuits either, because she wouldn't be there for lights out. She saw Jo and Alison waiting for her at the end of the school hall.

'Boring,' she mouthed just as the bell went for the end of break.

She helped to put the stock away in the cupboard and strolled over to the door and leant against the wall with Jo and Alison, hitching her skirt up an extra inch and loosening her tie and the buttons on her school blouse.

"Did you see the new girl?" Alison asked. "She's a full boarder."

"Poor thing," Melanie said, a touch of sympathy creeping in to her response. Melanie was a day girl. Her mother collected her in the Rover outside the school gates after her violin lesson or optional Spanish tutorial. Sometimes Alison and Jo came to the farm for tea, with the family; Melanie's mother and father and two older brothers. They had to get written permission from Matron on a school day who would try to find some reason why they couldn't go. Eventually she would capitulate after she had received a promise of a lift back from Mrs Melrose for 9pm.

Melanie liked her name, Melanie Melrose, she hoped to be famous one day and it had a ring to it. She wasn't sure whether she wanted to be a violinist, she was already on Grade 4 and flung her long blonde hair behind her when she played. Or maybe she would be in the Olympics, she was good at most sports. She knew Jo would have liked to be top at something, although to give her her due, she was a good all rounder.

Jo always looked adoringly at her, it was nice to be adored.

Jo liked the games lessons and it was hockey today. She liked to play on the wing because she was a fast runner. Melanie usually played centre because she was tall and did a great bully-off.

Jo paraded around the changing room in her new

bra, it was a 32A. It was white and lacy. "Mummy bought it for me at the weekend. It's got wired support," she demonstrated to her classmates, lifting her small breasts in her hands. She didn't have a cleavage like Melanie, but she did have matching frilly white knickers under the regulation school bloomers. She always came back with new things after a weekend at home. Jo's mum worked in fashion in London.

Alison only came back with a tuck box, or a new cardigan or something if she had grown out of her old one. She and Alison were weekly boarders, which usually meant that parents commuted to and from the City during the week, collected the girls on Fridays and brought them back on Sunday evenings after the weekend. Over the past few weeks though, Alison had been staying at school. Something to do with her Dad working weekends.

The games mistress came into the changing rooms to hurry them along. Jo quickly put on her green games kit, pushing the shin pads under the thick knee length socks.

The new girl, Freya, was struggling to get her games kit out of her kit bag. Jo watched from under her fringe as Freya tied the laces on her hockey boots. She didn't want to watch her too closely as one of the girls had called her queer last week. Freya was shuffling awkwardly into an aertex blouse and games skirt. How embarrassing; it was navy blue not green.

Freya pushed herself into the seat at the corner table in the library. Thankfully she had a free lesson now.

She reached up to get some books from the shelves above and spread them out on the table so that no one would sit opposite, then put her satchel on the chair next to her. She took a deep breath, forcing the tears back and swallowing down the lump in her throat. She put her head in her hands, "Elohim ya'azor li," she whispered.

She took an envelope out of her pocket and opened a crumpled letter, stroking it out on the desk in front of her. She traced the beautiful writing with her fingertips and read the three pages of vellum through again, for the hundredth time. Her brother David Tarski was just 13 and due to have his Bar-Mitzvah in summer. Her parents had delayed the happy occasion so that the family could get back together in Kiev in the summer. Another term of this mishmar.

She was only a year older than him, she was so close to him. They talked about family and friends, shifting between the English and Yiddish vocabulary, using Jewish terms of endearment. Somehow they were more meaningful than the broken sharp words used in the English language.

"Shalom Freya ..." he went on to talk of his lessons at the school, a walking distance from the family home. He had increased his study of the Torah. He talked of their eldest brother now working with his father in Manhattan, a lawyer for the Jewish community. They were all planning to leave Kiev and join him in time, when the family business had increased still further. Her older sister was very domesticated, using only kosher food and bringing her own little boy round to see their mother almost on a daily basis. And young Daniela, their own sister, was nine years of age last week. Muter still treated her as her baby of the family, even though she now had a grandson.

He prayed to HaShem, he continued, in the hope that she had settled into this school better than the last. He knew their parents wanted the best education for them all and had only her interest at heart. So he prayed and prayed she would find peace and friendship with the other girls and would be allowed to join in school assembly this time instead of standing in the corridor. Wasn't it a multi-faith school after all?

Daniela sent a kush to land on her cheek.

Ahava, as always – David.

Freya looked across the library hiding her tear-filled eyes behind her thick glasses. The rude girl Alison was sitting with her bag on the table propping her head on it and looking at her watch. Freya edged sideways in her chair so that she wouldn't be in her line of sight. She took out her fountain pen and some notepaper from her bag and started to write back, framing the words and letters into beautiful shapes on the page.

Alison had been watching the clock on the library wall and checking her wristwatch every five minutes. It was 4 o'clock and the school bell went for the end of the day. She grabbed her satchel and pushed her way through the girls leaving the library. She ran down the stairs and along the corridor making her way to the science lab. First in, she sat on the front bench just in front of his desk.

Mr Kettering looked up from his notes and smiled at her.

Alison's heart fluttered, could he be feeling the same for her as she felt for him?

After all, he always found time for her, when she demanded his attention.

She had been doing much better in Chemistry too, getting better marks and higher grades.

She'd been trying so hard to have something in common, so that he could be proud of her.

"Good afternoon Alison, the Periodic Table it is. Have you got your chart out so we can go over it?"

"Good afternoon Sir," should she call him by his first name now?

"Now then let me explain, all the elements in Group 1A are alkali metals on the left, then right across to the other side for rare earth elements."

"And elements in the same group are similar to each other, Sir." She asked, opening her satchel and getting her pen and chart out. She pointed to the tables laid out in front of her.

He left his chair and started to walk round to her bench.

OMG – she was so glad she had borrowed Jo's deodorant, her heart was beating so fast, the problem was – he was married, but maybe if he realised what he meant to her he would overlook that fact, although it did give her an uncomfortable feeling, a bit, him already having a wife.

He had reached the back of her chair.

Oh shit, some of the other girls from 3B were coming in to the lab, that would mean she would have to wait and linger around at the end of the tutorial just to get his attention again.

"Please Sir, I think I've got the hang of it now," she said, waving her pen in the air to pull his attention back to her.

He laughed and leant over her shoulder, straightening out the periodic tables a little more.

This was it, all the other girls would be so jealous when they realised his feelings for her.

"Alison! You are so demanding! You are just like my three year old daughter."

Daughter? Surely not. He must mean wife. You are just like my wife, surely he meant you are just like my wife.

"The main groups are numbered 1 – 7 going from left to right . . .and …"

Alison caught a lump in her throat and looked down, she felt so stupid, the symbols on the periodic table swam before her eyes.

In the dormitory **Jo** put on her pyjamas and walked over to **Alison**, passing her a biscuit from the stash given to her by **Melanie** at break time. She nudged her, sniggered loudly, casting a look in **Freya**'s direction.

Freya was looking down as she changed into her thick woollen nightdress. Her face was ashen. She was holding her petticoat and pants away from herself at arms length, as if they didn't belong to her. Her face was petrified as she looked at the red-brown stains covering her clothing.

Alison stood a moment longer – looking from left to right, at Freya and Jo and at the other girls around the room. Time stood still. Then slowly she knelt down and pulled her games kit out from under the bed. She took out two bulky white pads and passed them to Freya, touching her hand as she did so.

"You'll need these now," she said very gently. "It's called 'Becoming a Woman'. It hurts a lot at times and sometimes it's all a bit confusing, but you'll get used to it. We all have to in the end."

THE SPONGE

It was hot, the temperature scorched my body. I moved this way and that in the burning water, searching for a cooler place to shelter, to hide. The chemicals invaded my cells. I tried to filter them, for I knew they would destroy the bacteria I needed to survive.

The bath was helping. The soothing aroma of jasmine filtered through the steam filled room. Jasmine; their favourite smell, as they had walked the cobbled streets, lined with Venetian buildings and overhanging bougainvillea.

The white blossoms delicately opening their soft insides allowing their scent to pervade courtyards and balconies in the dusk and early evening.

She slowly lifts me out of the water and rubs me across her body. I caress her arms and legs as I am expected to do and mould into the curves beneath her breasts. She lifts me to her lips brushing them against my limbs, then holds me higher and squeezes the water from my body with her fingers, lifting her face to receive the flow over her eyes and cheeks and mouth.

They had stopped in the courtyard café for a glass of wine from a copper filled carafe before wandering down to choose from the many restaurants along the seafront. He would take two chairs and bring them together under the overhanging vine, steadying the table with a geranium in a terracotta pot.

Stavros brought fresh figs and peaches on a plate, slipping back discreetly into the kitchens. The juices slipped from the fruit as he peeled back the skin and placed a slice between her lips.

They relaxed, hands held over the blue and white checked cloth with the sounds of the chirping crickets and waves lapping against the boats on the seashore.

I had been changed long before I had taken on the colour of her skin. I had been grey and coated in a tough protective layer. But when the diver used his knife to peel back my skin; I had bled, revealing my white blood and true nature. And he cut me from my source taking me from my very roots where I had lain since the beginning of time.

Katharina would usher them into her home to exhibit her new paintings; an oil on canvas, a deserted boat, or perhaps an urn on a table with a view out to the sea beyond. He would look at them from all angles, marvelling at the colours or the serenity the picture evoked. Knowing he could buy the same in any of the corner shops on the mainland, but still pressing twenty euros into her hand, exclaiming at his bargain, insisting.

We had been warned, the messages had passed between us, whispered from the remains of other sponges tossed carelessly back into the sea. Battered and bruised, these traumatised rejects recounted their tales of beatings and immersion in boiling water.

Occasionally we attempted to retaliate by sending out poisonous barbs and spitting our bile, but the traders were stronger and suited in diving gear and breathing machines. Death from paralysis no longer prevented them as it had in the times of our grandfathers.

Every year the locals threw their arms around them as if they were their own returned from distant shores, showering them with gifts of lemons, fresh oysters, a baked feta and olive pastry. Welcoming, encompassing.

They said they would buy a summer property here on this beautiful island, away from the mainland and usual crowds of sun seekers, it was their second home, their escape from reality.

We could do nothing. Once they knew of our presence, there was no escape. Our only hope was that they were compassionate and skilled enough to realise our extinction or existence depended upon an accurate slice of the knife. A root left behind could regenerate, begin a new colony; if there remained enough core, if only the cut had not been too deep.

They would stroll further, arms wrapped around each other, marvelling at the views from every turn in the road. Or pause and dance a few steps to the Greek music coming from the bars along the way.

Long ago, and before; I had danced with my brothers and sisters in the warm Aegean sea when the late afternoon sun trickled through the waters. The turquoise and gold fish played their games amongst my tentacles. As I caressed their bodies they fed me particles of algae and protozoa salvaged from the surface. At times I hid them; covering them with my limbs then pulling back to reveal them to the sea urchins and anemones who in turn played, tossing and tantalising with threats of stings and poison. Until they jerked their colourful bodies and swam away to nose at the crabs beneath the boulders.

They would eat late in the evening; fried aubergines, calamari and lamb baked to exquisite softness in hot clay ovens with vine tomatoes bursting in their roundness. He would lean to her and feed her his last morsel of rough bread torn from the loaf soaked in succulent herbs and lemon juices from his plate, telling her;

'What is mine – is yours.'

He would take her hands, interlocking her fingers, bringing her palm to his lips. She was his;

'Love. My angel from a place beyond time itself.'

Cut, we were thrown together in nets and dropped onto the wooden floorboards of the larger boats, gasping from the fall to the decks and lack of oxygen to our breathing mechanisms. We moulded our bodies around each other to absorb the pain, keeping the younger of our species to the centre.

Later, they celebrated long into the night with the ancient act of consummation; their arms and legs encircling one another, entwined as one, moving together with the flow, their cries mingling with the sounds of cicadas and night owls around them in the blackened sky.

On the shore, we were separated and prostrated in the baking sun then strung up and tied by our tentacles to a rope. At night, teasingly dipped into the mantle of the sea, only to be awoken the next day to repeated beatings from hardened wood, until every external membrane and tissue was broken leaving only the skeletal fibres and our spirit remaining within the cells. Barely alive wondering; what was the meaning, the reason, behind this torture.

They would change positions on the motorbike, he – pushed up hard against her as she revved the engine, taking the sharp gravelled corners at speed in the dry day time heat.

They would stop, prop the bike against an olive tree and contemplate a church on a hilltop, its blue and white domed roof reaching to the cloudless sky above. She would cover her head and shoulders with the scarf at the door. He would put coins into the ancient brass box, always lighting a candle before moving to the front without her and dropping to his knees with the sign of the cross. He never told her what he prayed for as she looked at the icons and gifts of toys, lace and rushes around the simple benches.

Sometimes he cried, she didn't ask why. It could have been the sadness or simply the eternal beauty was too much to bear.

We were put in order and displayed on the roadsides next to the crosses in their glass boxes. People stopped and passed us around, squeezing and moulding our bodies, feeling our weight and measuring our girth.

Those less lucky were penned into crates and taken to factories, or foreign shores past the watching old women with their pipes. There the beatings and bleaching would start again, their bodies raked, brushed and moulded into the required shape. We heard their screams within.

He had chosen the sponge from the roadside looking deeply into its holy depth, matching and moulding it against her sun-kissed body.

'They are said to have healing properties,' he had said, as he held it, then bent to brush her lips with his own and put his hand behind her head tangling his fingers in her long hair.

She didn't see the frown cross his face as he turned away and held his stomach. She didn't hear him retch into the toilet behind the supermarket. She didn't see him struggle to lift his arm to dim the blinding headache which had become more severe, more frequent of late.

He poured her a glass of wine and they sat in the quiet evening, looking at the sunset from their balcony overlooking the bay. The boats tinkled their messages of hope for the next day's harvest.

They were preparing to journey. I was squeezed into the case with plastic bottles of chemicals by my side. The lid was shut and I was trapped in the darkness.

He died that night. The mourners in black had held onto her as she screamed and wailed tearing at her hair and clothes, following the procession through the streets to the little church on the top of the hill. He had been placed in an open coffin, they gathered around him dropping flowers, reed crosses and hand sewn handkerchiefs at his feet. Men and women alike knelt to kiss his head and touch his hands held together in prayer. They made the shape of the cross to the altar and placed artefacts around the church on every bench and window ledge. They wept with her, sharing her pain, delaying her departure, making her one of them.

She bends and rolls me in her hands as the warm water grows colder around her. I take the shape she puts me in, go to the places to clean her and refresh her and stay by her side. As I caress her face, she rewards me with salted water from the ducts in her eyes. Occasionally she will breathe with me sucking the water in – and out – of my filaments without thinking. Then she will leave the cold bath, withdrawing her long legs and towel her damp hair, far away in her eyes. She will rinse me out in cool clean water gently squeezing the excess from my body and place me in a shell by the bath.

She wanted to die with him. He filled her very soul. Around her and in her. She had been ripped apart. Her heart torn out. She lifts her head and silently screams from within.

I will stay to my own end to bathe her and heal her and soak up her pain. I will stay to give her back her life, for that is what I am called to do, from my core. I know the pain she has deep within the very centre of her, alone now in the other life. She is not so developed in her time as I. She has not felt the vastness of the oceans. She does not know she will grow again, in time, from her roots and his spirit deep within her cells.